My Little Brave Girl

By **Hilary Duff**

Illustrations by
Kelsey Garrity-Riley

Random House New York

The world is big, my little brave girl.

It's all here for you.

Love is vast, my little brave girl,

and yours is endless.

The sun burns bright, my little brave girl,
and you will find the light.

The stars are high, and you can reach them.

Oceans run deep,
and you will learn to swim.

The days will come and go,
and you will learn to count.

Flavors will dance across your tongue,
my little brave girl, and you will enjoy
the delicious adventure.

Your feet will take many big steps, my little brave girl.

Let your heart lead the way.

Kindness is the way
the world goes round.

And you can
spin and spin.

Your mind is all your own,
my little brave girl,
and you will discover
how special you are.

Now dream without borders,
my little brave girl.
Your future knows no bounds.

For Luca, who taught me all of the unimaginable
love that a mother gets to have.

And for Banks, who inspired this book. The cliché of not
being able to love another child as much as the first felt
so real, and you completely proved me wrong.

Also for all brave littles and bigs across the globe. —HD

• • •

To Mom and Dad, with love —KGR

All rights reserved. Published in the United States by Random House Children's Books,
a division of Penguin Random House LLC, New York.

Random House and the colophon are registered trademarks of Penguin Random House LLC.

Visit us on the Web! rhcbooks.com

Educators and librarians, for a variety of teaching tools, visit us at RHTeachersLibrarians.com

Library of Congress Cataloging-in-Publication Data is available upon request.
ISBN 978-0-593-30072-5 (trade) — ISBN 978-0-593-30073-2 (lib. bdg.) —
ISBN 978-0-593-30074-9 (ebook)

This book is set in 18-point YWFT Mullino.

Book design by Nicole Gastonguay

MANUFACTURED IN CHINA
10 9 8 7 6 5 4 3 2 1
First Edition